Short Tales
NATIVE AMERICAN MYTHS
STOLEN FIRE
A SEMINOLE TRICKSTER MYTH

Adapted by Anita Yasuda
Illustrated by Estudio Haus

magic
wagon

visit us at www.abdopublishing.com

Published by Magic Wagon, a division of the ABDO Group, PO Box 398166, Minneapolis, MN 55439. Copyright © 2013 by Abdo Consulting Group, Inc. International copyrights reserved in all countries. All rights reserved. No part of this book may be reproduced in any form without written permission from the publisher.

Short Tales™ is a trademark and logo of Magic Wagon.

Printed in the United States of America, North Mankato, Minnesota.
052012
092012

Adapted text by Anita Yasuda
Illustrations by Estudio Haus
Edited by Rebecca Felix
Series design by Craig Hinton

Design elements: Diana Walters/iStockphoto

Library of Congress Cataloging-in-Publication Data
Yasuda, Anita.
 Stolen fire : a Seminole trickster myth / by Anita Yasuda ; illustrated by Estudio Haus.
    p. cm. -- (Short tales Native American myths)
  ISBN 978-1-61641-883-0
 1. Seminole Indians--Folklore. 2. Seminole mythology. I. Estudio Haus (Firm) II. Title.
 E99.S28Y37 2012
 398.2089'973859--dc23
                        2012004697

MYTHICAL CHARACTERS

THE RABBIT

A mischievous trickster character
in Seminole folklore

MEDICINE MEN

Wise members of the Seminole tribe
who make magic

INTRODUCTION

This legend comes from the Seminole people. In the mid-1700s, the Seminole migrated to the present-day state of Florida. Seminole myths and legends are an important way for customs and histories to be passed through the generations.

Stolen Fire comes from a collection of Seminole myths compiled by the Federal Writers' Project of the Works Progress Administration for the State of Florida in 1939. The legend reflects the Seminole belief that animals are important in helping humans to live good lives. The rabbit is mischievous to the Seminole, but he helped people survive on Earth by bringing them fire. The Green Corn Dance in the story is an annual Seminole ceremony held in the spring around a central fire.

Many, many moons ago, fire came to Earth. It flickered and glowed. It crackled and hissed. Only one Native American tribe was lucky enough to learn the secret of this fire.

Other tribes went to this tribe saying, "Please give us fire. We want it so badly."

But the tribe with fire refused, saying, "We will not share our fire."

The tribe with fire guarded their secret carefully.

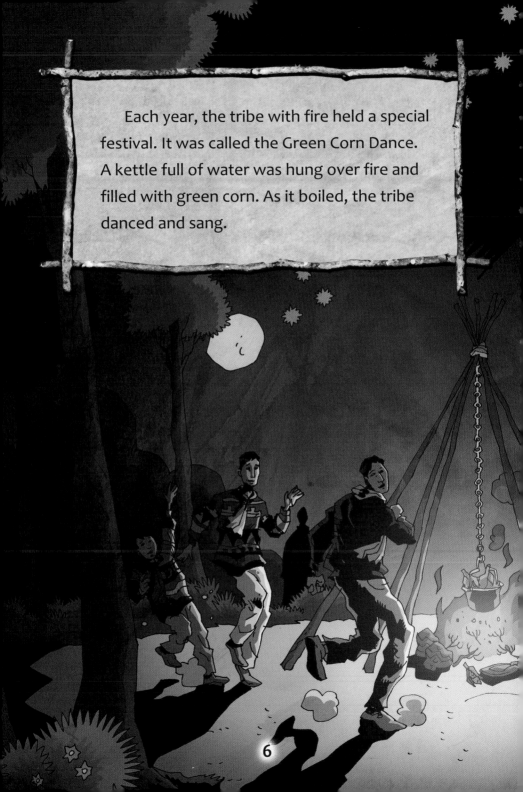

Each year, the tribe with fire held a special festival. It was called the Green Corn Dance. A kettle full of water was hung over fire and filled with green corn. As it boiled, the tribe danced and sang.

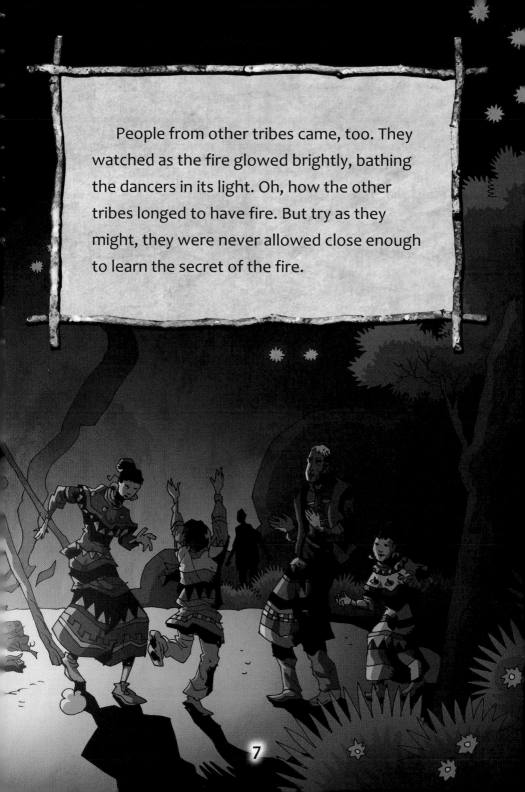

People from other tribes came, too. They watched as the fire glowed brightly, bathing the dancers in its light. Oh, how the other tribes longed to have fire. But try as they might, they were never allowed close enough to learn the secret of the fire.

To one Green Corn Dance came a rabbit. He was the biggest, finest, and handsomest rabbit the people had ever seen.

"Please, may I not dance around the fire with you?" the rabbit begged.

The dancers refused to let him.

The rabbit began to sing.

"Why, he sings sweeter than anyone," one man said.

The rabbit began to dance.

"Why, he dances better than anyone," another said.

The rabbit began to whoop.

"Why, he whoops better than anyone," more said.

The elders began to worry.

"This rabbit is not what he says he is," the first elder said.

"I agree," the second elder said, looking at the rabbit.

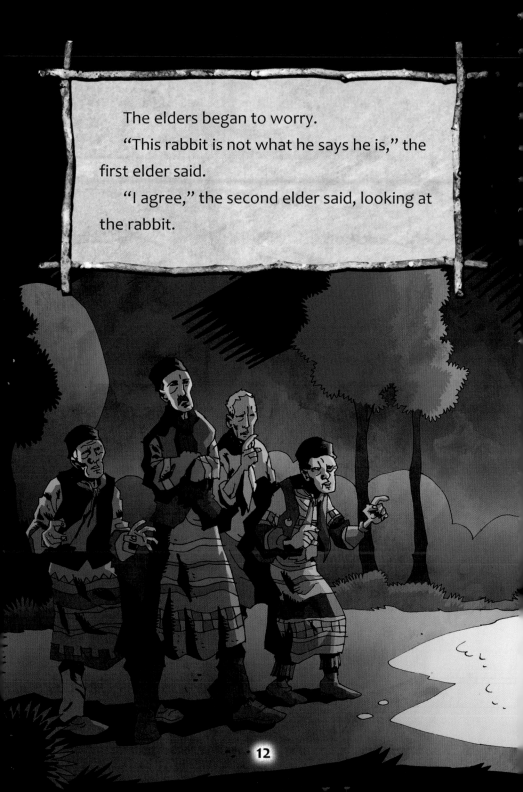

The elders suspected that the rabbit was in disguise.

"He is not a rabbit but a man from another tribe," the third elder said.

"Beware!" the fourth elder said. "He wants to steal our fire."

The elders tried to warn the young people. They repeated, "That rabbit wants to steal our fire."

But the young people did not listen to their elders.

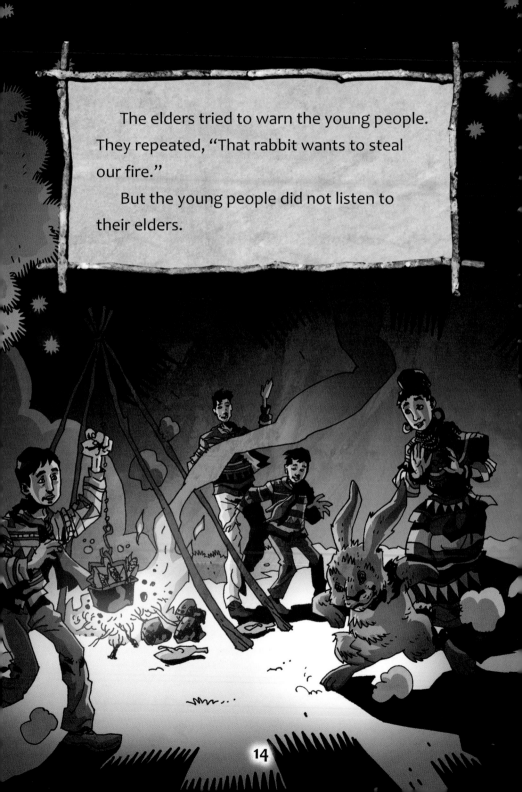

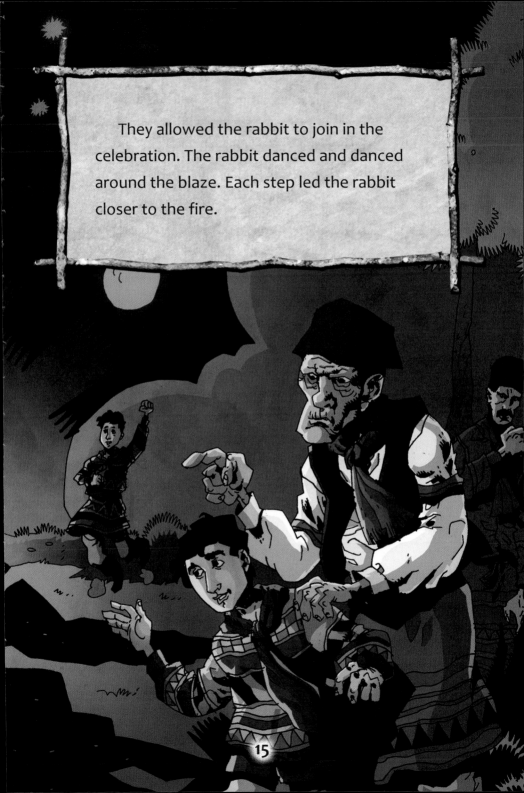

They allowed the rabbit to join in the celebration. The rabbit danced and danced around the blaze. Each step led the rabbit closer to the fire.

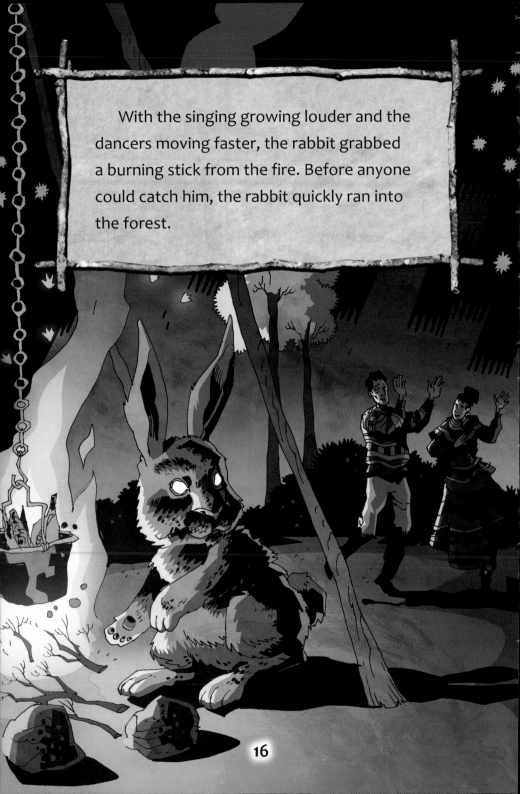

With the singing growing louder and the dancers moving faster, the rabbit grabbed a burning stick from the fire. Before anyone could catch him, the rabbit quickly ran into the forest.

The people were upset watching him go. They did not want the rabbit to have fire. The tribe held a council.

"We will bring rain. This will put out the rabbit's fire," said the wise medicine men.

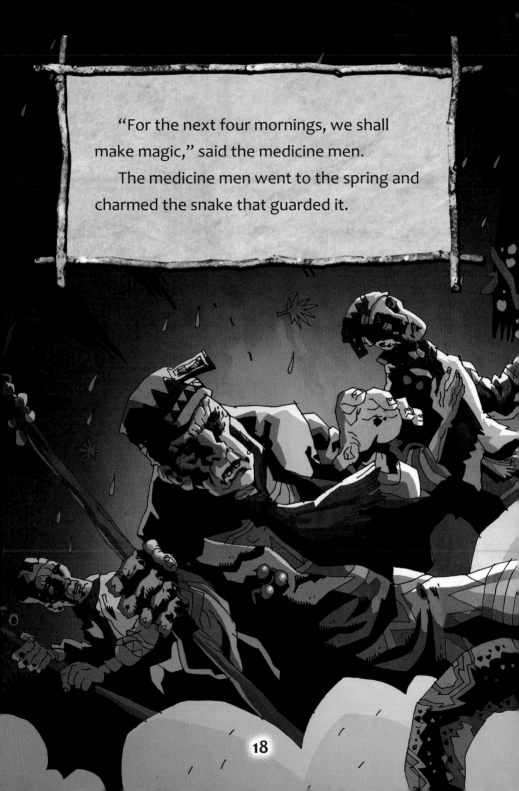

"For the next four mornings, we shall make magic," said the medicine men.

The medicine men went to the spring and charmed the snake that guarded it.

The ground trembled and branches swayed. Light flashed across the sky. Suddenly, rain burst from the clouds. The medicine men's magic had worked.

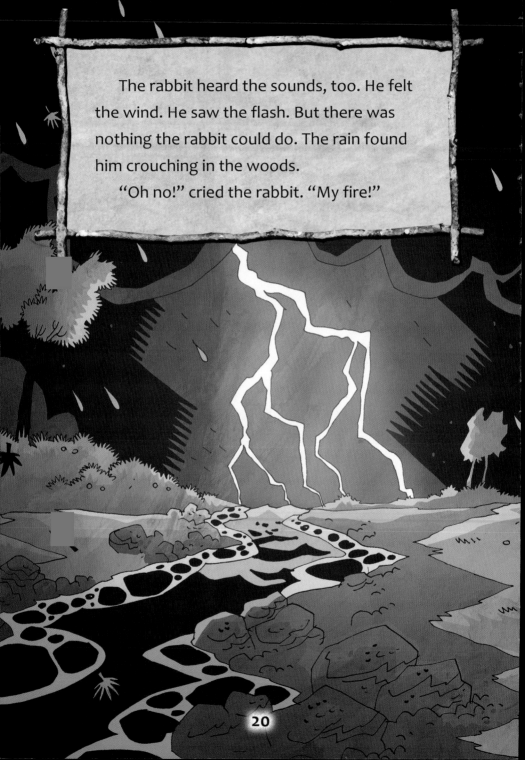

The rabbit heard the sounds, too. He felt the wind. He saw the flash. But there was nothing the rabbit could do. The rain found him crouching in the woods.

"Oh no!" cried the rabbit. "My fire!"

The medicine men's magic was powerful. It rained and rained until the rabbit's precious fire stick went out.

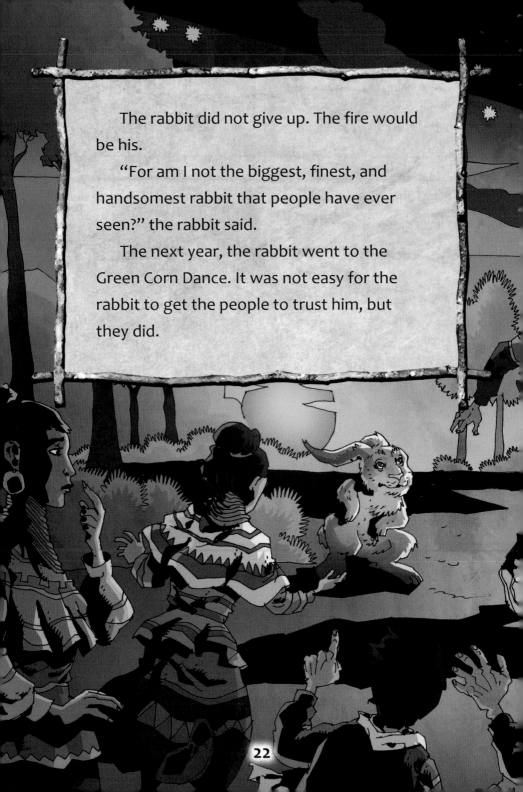

The rabbit did not give up. The fire would be his.

"For am I not the biggest, finest, and handsomest rabbit that people have ever seen?" the rabbit said.

The next year, the rabbit went to the Green Corn Dance. It was not easy for the rabbit to get the people to trust him, but they did.

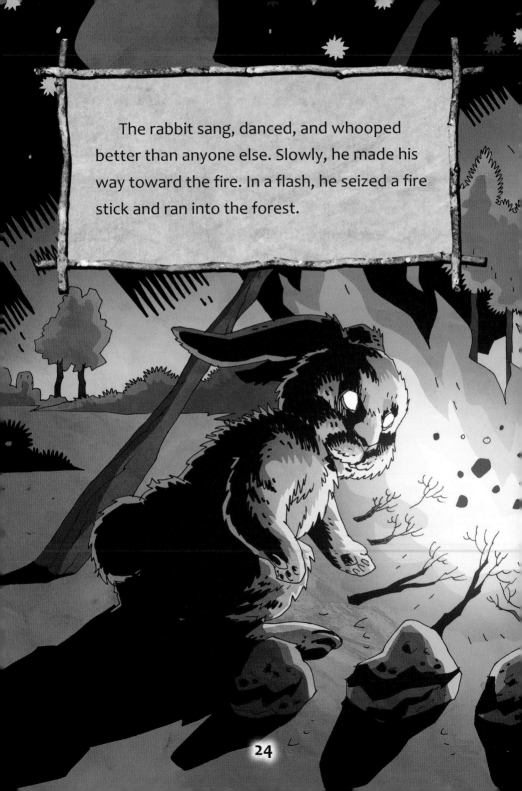

The rabbit sang, danced, and whooped better than anyone else. Slowly, he made his way toward the fire. In a flash, he seized a fire stick and ran into the forest.

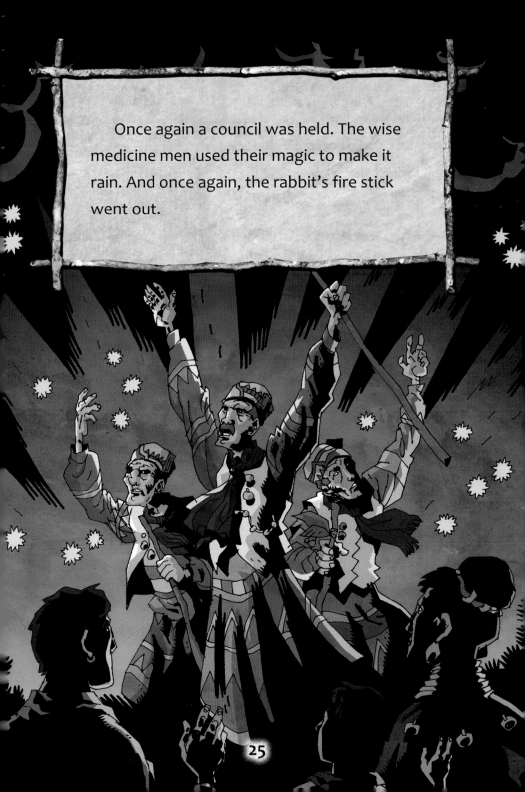

Once again a council was held. The wise medicine men used their magic to make it rain. And once again, the rabbit's fire stick went out.

The rabbit did not give up. The fire would be his.

"For am I not the biggest, finest, and handsomest rabbit that people have ever seen?" the rabbit said.

At his third Green Corn Dance, it was not easy for the rabbit to get people to trust him again, but they did. The rabbit sang. He danced. And he whooped better than anyone else.

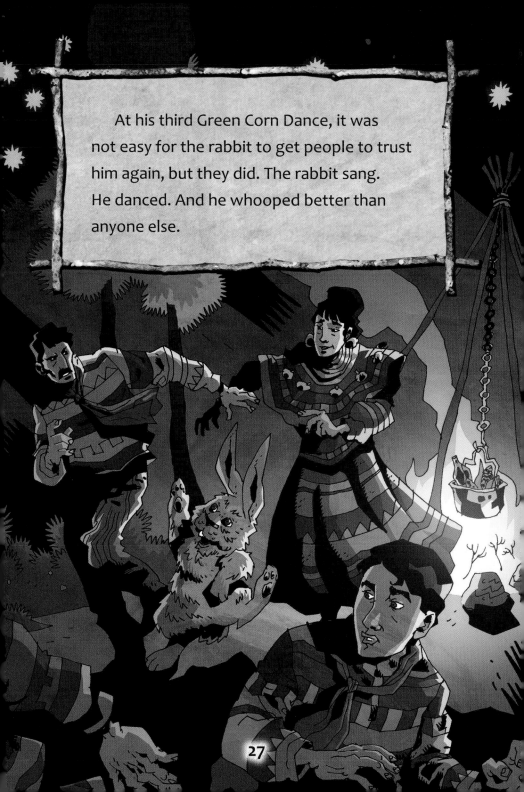

The rabbit slowly made his way toward the fire. In a flash, he seized a fire stick and ran into the forest.

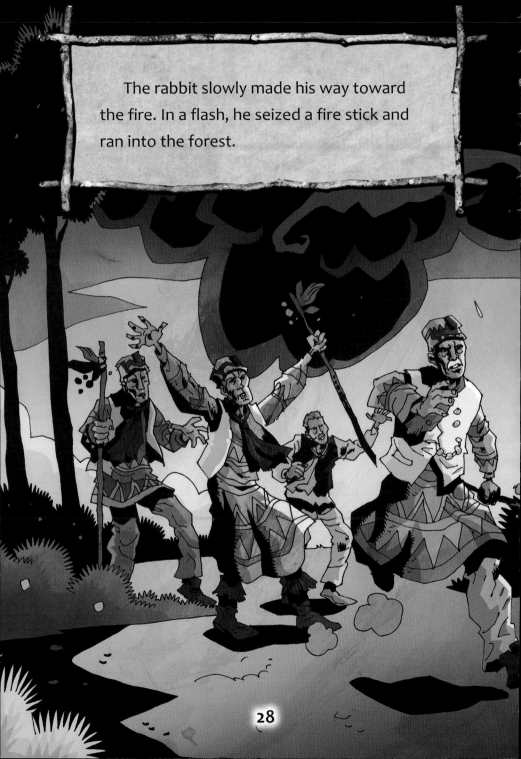

Once again a council was held. Once again the wise medicine men called upon their magic to make it rain. And once again, the rabbit's fire stick went out.

At his fourth Green Corn Dance, the rabbit was much wiser. This time when he grabbed a fire stick, the rabbit did not run into the forest.

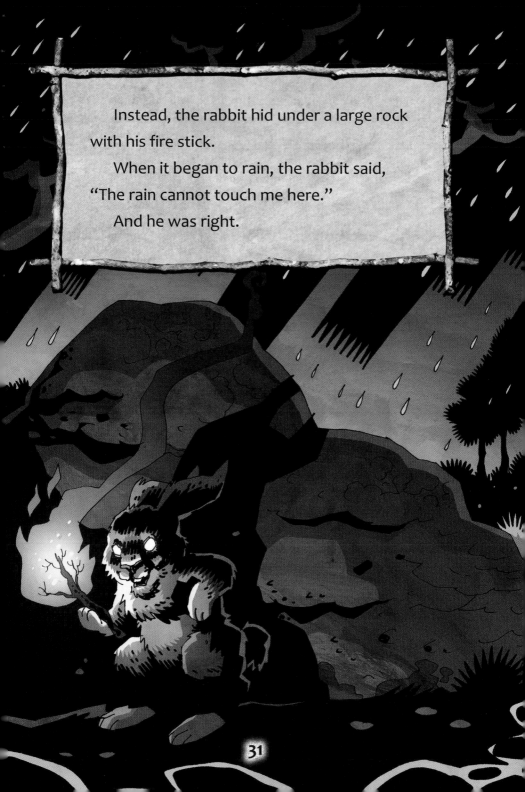

Instead, the rabbit hid under a large rock with his fire stick.

When it began to rain, the rabbit said, "The rain cannot touch me here."

And he was right.

When the rain stopped, the rabbit came out. His fire stick was still burning brightly.

"My fire is safe!" cried the rabbit. "Now, I will give it to everyone."

And this is how all Native American tribes learned the secret of fire.